Published by Brimax Books, Newmarket, England 1993.
Printed in France by Pollina, 85400 Luçon - n° 16543

Read by Yourself

Illustrated by Angela Mills

BRIMAX · NEWMARKET · ENGLAND

Jumping Jack

by Geoffrey Alan
Illustrated by Angela Mills

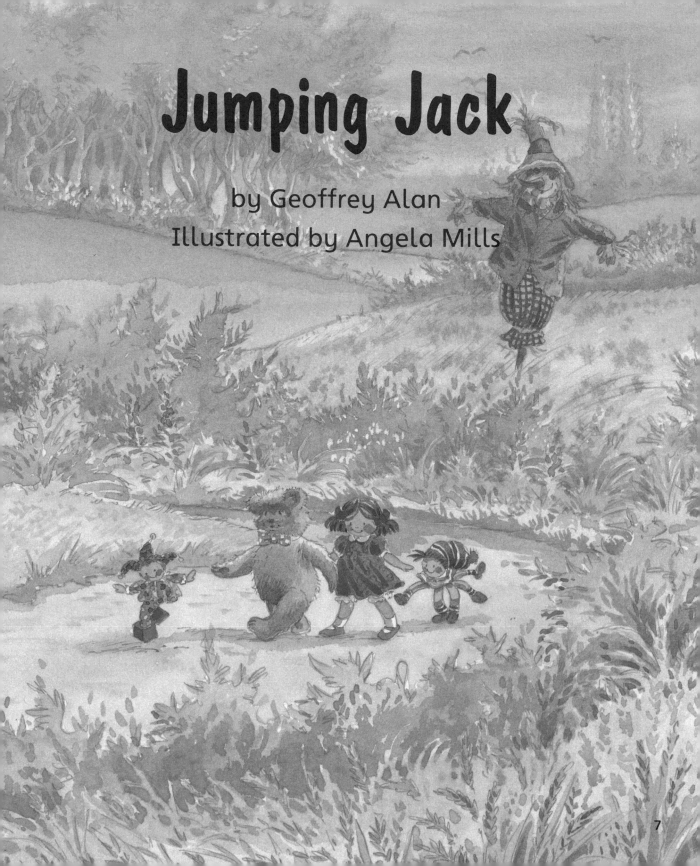

"I feel full of bounce today!" says Jack-in-the-box as he springs out from the toybox and bounces around the room. "Please be careful!" says Polly the Ragdoll. "Slow down, Jack!" call Oscar the Octopus and Tumble the Teddy Bear.

The toys belong to a little girl called Katy. She has gone away with her parents. Boing! Boing! Boing! Jack keeps on bouncing. Polly has found one of Katy's ribbons and is skipping with it. But Jack bounces too close to her and poor Polly is all tangled up.

"Come back and help me," Polly calls to Jack.

"All right!" he says. But Jack does not see Tumble trying to ride Katy's scooter.

"Look out!" shouts Tumble.

"Oh no!" says Jack. He bounces extra hard and springs right over the scooter. But Tumble wobbles and then falls off.

"Oops!" he says, landing on a bean-bag.

13

The bean-bag bursts and all
the little beans spill out.
"Oh no!" says Polly. "We will
have to put them all back and
sew it up again. You are a
pest, Jack!"
"No I am not," says Jack. "I
am only bouncing around!"
This time he lands on the end
of Katy's see-saw. On the
other end is a big cushion.
It flies through the air.

"Catch that cushion, someone," Jack laughs. But it lands on the book shelf and the books begin to slide off.

"Oh no!" yells Tumble, diving under a desk.

Polly puts up an umbrella. But as the books fall, Oscar catches them all at once.

"There is not enough room in here for you to be such a pest," he tells Jack.

"You are right!" says Jack.
He bounces over to the door,
springs up and opens it and
bounces outside.
"We had better follow him to
make sure that he does not
cause any trouble!" says
Oscar.
Boing! Splash! Boing! Splash!
It has been raining and Jack
bounces in and out of the
puddles along the path.

19

"This is fun," laughs Jack.
"Wait!" Polly calls after him.
She is still carrying her
umbrella.
"Where are you going, Jack?"
calls Oscar.
Jack does not hear his friends
calling him. He keeps on
bouncing along the path
beside the field.

Boing! Boing! Jack bounces
faster and faster.
A rabbit hops across the path
in front of him.
"Look at that!" says Jack.
"He can jump almost as high as
I can!"
Jack is not watching where he
is going, for he turns around
and bumps into the strangest
man he has ever seen.

Jack springs back in surprise and lands in the middle of the ditch. SPLAT! It is full of sticky mud. Jack tries to bounce out, but he is stuck. "Please help me out of here!" he cries to his three friends. "How did you get in there?" asks Oscar.
"He made me jump!" says Jack. "Look!"

"He is only a scarecrow!" chuckles Oscar.

"You should not have bounced off like that," says Tumble.

"Well I cannot bounce anywhere now," says Jack sadly.

Tumble nearly falls in the ditch. "The sides are very slippery," he says.

"Then how can we rescue Jack?" asks Polly. Oscar sees her umbrella and has an idea.

Oscar wraps six of his long legs around a nearby tree. Then he stretches out the other two.

"I'll hold onto you, Polly," he says. "And you can hold on to Tumble."

"What shall I do?" asks Tumble puzzled.

"You can hold onto Polly's umbrella and give the other end to Jack," says Oscar.

Tumble is not sure that the plan will work. But they stretch out in a line, Polly holds onto Tumble with both hands.

"Grab the handle, Jack!" says Tumble. "Now all together . . . Pull!"

They all pull very hard.

At last, Jack is free.

"Thank you!" he says. "I might have been stuck forever!"

"You will need to get scrubbed in the doll's-house bathroom," says Polly. "You are very muddy!"

"I am very sorry, too," says Jack. "I promise never to be a pest again."

Say these words again

bounce	springs
tangled	extra
wobbles	sew
enough	beside
faster	across
tries	slippery

What can you see?

scooter

bean-bag

see-saw

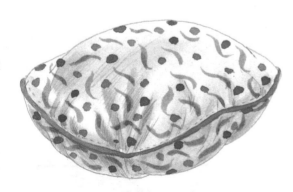

cushion

scarecrow

Animals' party

by Hilary Lazell

Illustrated by Angela Mills

Harry Hippo lives deep in the jungle. He is a very kind, friendly hippo but he is also the dirtiest, smelliest animal in the jungle. Whenever it is time to bathe in the lake, Harry runs the other way. His mother is in despair.

"I do not know what to do with Harry," she says to Mrs Giraffe.
"I do not think he likes water."
Harry does not like water.
"It is too wet and cold," he moans as his mother tucks him up in bed.

"If you do not have a bath soon, no-one will play with you," warns his mother. "In fact, no-one will know who you are, you are covered in so much mud."
She holds her nose and kisses him goodnight. He really is far too smelly to be near.

There is one type of bath that Harry likes and that is a mud bath. When he is tired of playing with his friends or when they are tired of the smell, Harry goes to a mud hole and rolls over in the slimy mud until he is covered from head to foot. Needless to say, swarms of flies follow him home, but everyone else stays out of his way.

One day, Harry finds all his friends whispering excitedly. "Ssh. Here comes Harry," says Eric Elephant. All the animals run off.
"I wonder what all that is about," says Harry.

Later he finds his friends'
mothers whispering together.
"Ssh. Here comes Harry," says
Mrs Tiger. They all rush off
to get their children for
their baths.
When Harry reaches home he
tells his mother how strangely
the other animals have been
acting.

"I think they are planning a surprise," says Harry. "I love surprises." He is too tired to notice the worried look on his mother's face, and he falls asleep dreaming about what the surprise can be. The next day Harry meets some of his friends.

"Sorry we cannot play, we have to get ready for the party," they say. And they all run off.

So that is the surprise. But no-one has told Harry to get ready! Where is the party being held? Harry heads to his mud hole.

Just past the lake in the big clearing, hanging between two trees, is a 'WELCOME TO THE PARTY' banner. Harry cannot believe his eyes. There are hundreds of balloons and tables full of food. Just as he is near enough to smell the food, someone comes rushing up to him. It is Granny Elephant.

"Go away! Shoo! You nasty, smelly object! Do not go near the party food! Now be off with you!" And she chases poor Harry away from the clearing. Harry runs as fast as his legs will carry him, tears streaming down his face.

He has not been invited to the party. No-one wants him there. Harry flops down on the grass and sobs enormous wet tears. A long time and many tears later Harry stands up, shakes himself dry and wanders miserably on, not noticing in which direction he is going.

Before he realises it he is back at the clearing where the party is.

"Look! It is Harry!" cries someone. "And he is clean!" Everyone rushes over.

"Well done! You look quite handsome," says Gerry Giraffe. Harry looks at his reflection in the lake. It is true, he is clean! All his tears have washed the dirt away!

Harry's mother comes up behind him. "I am proud of you, Harry," she whispers. Harry glows with happiness. Now that he is clean he can join the party. Later, as he tucks into his third bowl of cake and ice-cream, Harry promises that he will never go near a mud hole again. Well not for a few days, anyway!

Say these words again

friendly	smelliest
really	covered
swarms	whispering
strangely	dreaming
surprise	between
chases	handsome

Who can you see?

Harry Hippo

Eric Elephant

Mrs Tiger

Granny Elephant

Gerry Giraffe 65

The naughty kitten

by Frances Kendle

Illustrated by Angela Mills

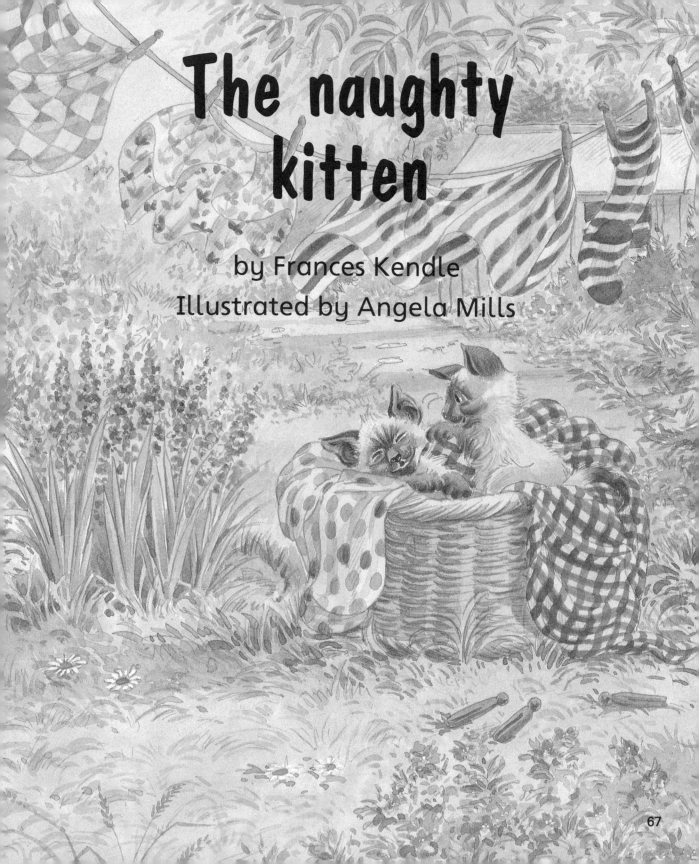

Ching and Chang are two Siamese kittens who love exploring the garden. Everything has to be sniffed and anything that moves has to be chased. The trouble is that Chang is always getting into mischief.

Hardly a day goes by when he does not do something naughty. But because they look so much alike, Chang makes sure it is Ching who gets the blame. One afternoon, after taking a nap, Chang leaps out of their basket.

"Come on Ching," he says excitedly. "Let's go and have some fun."

"I'm not going out anymore," says Ching. "I had to go without my cream at lunchtime because of you."

"Please yourself," says Chang, and he scampers off.

Ching curls up and tries to get back to sleep, but he cannot so he sets off to find his brother. To his surprise Chang is sitting quietly beside the garden pond washing his face. For once he is behaving himself.

Ching hurries to join him.
As he draws nearer, he sees
something that makes his fur
stand on end. A glance in the
pond and Ching's fears are
confirmed. Oscar's ball is in
the pond! Oscar is a big dog
who lives in the same house
as the kittens, but he does not
like them one little bit. The
ball in the pond is the thing
Oscar loves most in the world.

"Ch . . Ch . . Chang," Ching stammers. "What have you done?" Chang stops washing and glances innocently at his shaking brother. "What is the matter? I have not done anything," he replies. Ching looks again at the pond.

"But you have," Ching insists. "Oscar's ball is in the pond," he says in horror.

"What ball?" says crafty Chang. "I have not seen any ball," he grins. Then he shoots off and hides in the bushes.

Poor Ching is so worried about getting the blame that he feels like running away and never coming back. He gazes in despair at the pond, he does not know what to do. Then suddenly he has an idea. Ching knows that his brother is a very good swimmer and he decides to play a trick on him.

"Chang! Chang! Come quickly!" he bellows. "There is something horrible in our pond!" Ching knows that his brother is not only naughty but very nosey as well. Almost at once Chang leaves his hiding place and bounds across the grass to look.

"Where?" he shouts and stares excitedly into the water. "Right near the edge," says Ching pretending to be afraid. Chang walks over to the edge of the pond and stoops for a closer look. Ching lifts his paw and gives him a shove. SPLASH! Chang falls into the water. A very wet and a very angry Chang climbs out of the pond.

The sight of his soaking wet
brother makes Ching roar with
laughter. A water lily is
stuck to his head and weeds
are hanging around his neck
and tripping him up as he walks.
"Oh dear!" laughs Ching, who
by now is lying on the grass
with his feet in the air.
Chang is very angry.

"What did you do that for?"
he shouts.
"Well, Oscar's ball is in the
water," says Ching.
"I know that. It fell in while
I was playing with it," says
Chang angrily.
"I know," Ching chuckles, "but
as the ball is in the water
and you are the kitten who is
wet, this time you will get
the blame."

Chang realises how clever his brother has been.

"So there is not anything horrible in the pond after all?" he asks.

"Not now", says Ching. "It just crawled out!" and taking to his heels he disappears behind the garden shed.

Say these words again

angry	mischief
afraid	scampers
surprise	naughty
something	horror
replies	suddenly
nosey	bounds

94

What did you see?

kittens

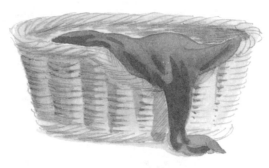

basket

ball

water lily

pond

Teddy Bear

by Patricia Chare

Illustrated by Angela Mills

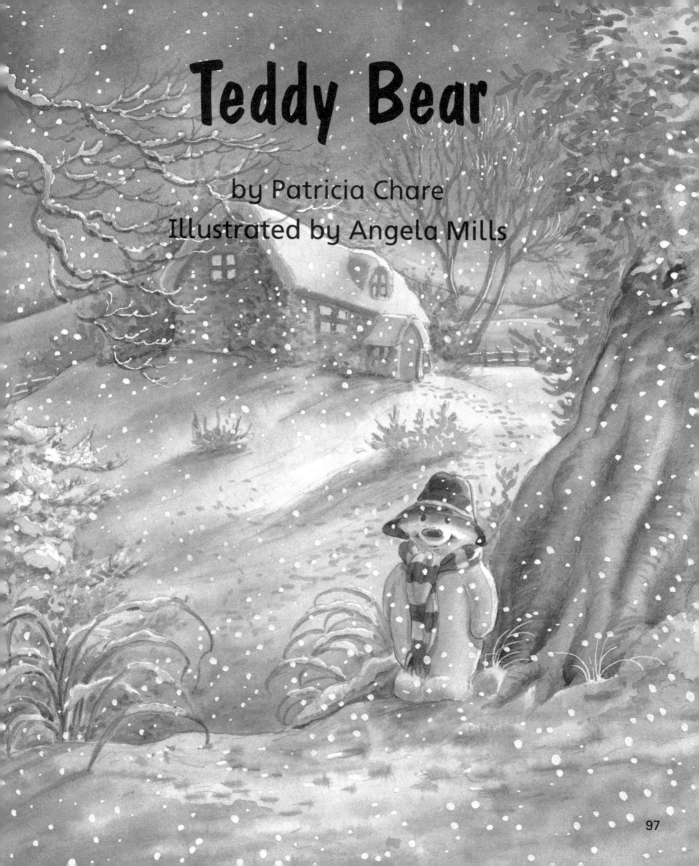

Teddy Bear wakes up. It is not time to get up yet. He looks at his clock and it is only six o'clock. He is warm and snug under his quilt but he knows that something is different about this morning. Something strange has happened, but he is not sure what.

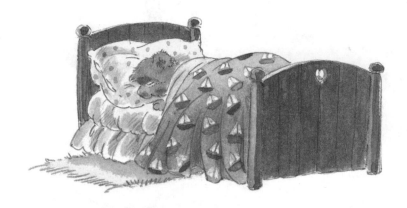

Teddy is afraid to move. What can be wrong? He creeps out of bed quietly, trying not to wake Sally. He tiptoes over to the window, stretches up high and looks out. What a sight!

The garden is all white, as though someone has put a blanket over it. He knows right away what it is, because he has read about it. It is snow! It had fallen silently while they were all asleep.

Teddy is very excited. He has never seen snow before. He shakes Sally and although she is only half awake she climbs out of bed. She goes over to the window to see what Teddy is pointing at. She rubs her eyes and looks out of the window. She gives a gasp of surprise!

"Oh Teddy!" she cries. "There is snow on the ground!"

Both Sally and Teddy are wide awake by now, and they want to go straight out into the snow. They go and wake their parents. Mother says that they must have some breakfast and put some warm clothes on first. They are so excited they cannot wait, but Father says they must.

They eat their breakfast very quickly and then put on their warmest clothes. Finally they are allowed to go outside. Sally stops on the doorstep. "Hurry up, Sally!" says Teddy, trying to get past her.

"No," says Sally. "I do not want to ruin the snow. It looks so lovely and smooth."

But Teddy does not mind. Out he goes — Crunch! Crunch! Crunch! He cannot stop. It is such good fun. He runs round and round making patterns in the snow. Teddy sees Spot the dog run out of the house. Spot has not seen snow before either.

Spot stands still and sniffs the cold, white stuff in surprise. His paws are cold. He puts his nose down into the snow and snuffles along trying to smell it. Whatever this is he does not like it. He goes back and sits on the doorstep, where he can keep his eye on things.

Teddy laughs at Spot and calls him over, but Spot will not move. Teddy can see a lump in the snow. What can it be?
He goes over to look. It is round. Teddy brushes some of the snow away. It is his ball.
The snow has covered it up!

"Should we build a snowman?"
says Sally.

"Oh yes!" cries Teddy. Their
father comes out to help them.
Building the snowman takes
a long time. Teddy is really
enjoying himself and although
it is a cold day, they are
very hot. Teddy is a bit
surprised about this, but his
father says it is because
they are all working so hard.

When they have finished the snowman, Mother brings out a hat and a scarf for him. They all think he looks very handsome. Sally says that he must have a name. They all suggest a few. Teddy wants to call him Teddy! They eventually decide on Edward.

"I'm cold," says Sally.
"So am I," says Teddy.
Now that they have stopped
working their toes and fingers
are starting to tingle, and
feel very cold. As they stand
looking at Edward the snowman,
Teddy can feel something very
strange touching his head. He
looks up into the sky. More
snow is falling!

The back door opens and Mother calls, "Come in now. I've made you some hot soup." They all rush inside to get warm. Mother makes them change into some dry, warm clothes before they can drink their soup. "I love soup," says Sally. "So do I," says Teddy. "But I love snow more!" And they all agree.

Say these words again

snug	different
sight	silently
pointing	awake
excited	allowed
outside	laughs
covered	finished

What can you see?

clock

dog

ball

soup

snowman